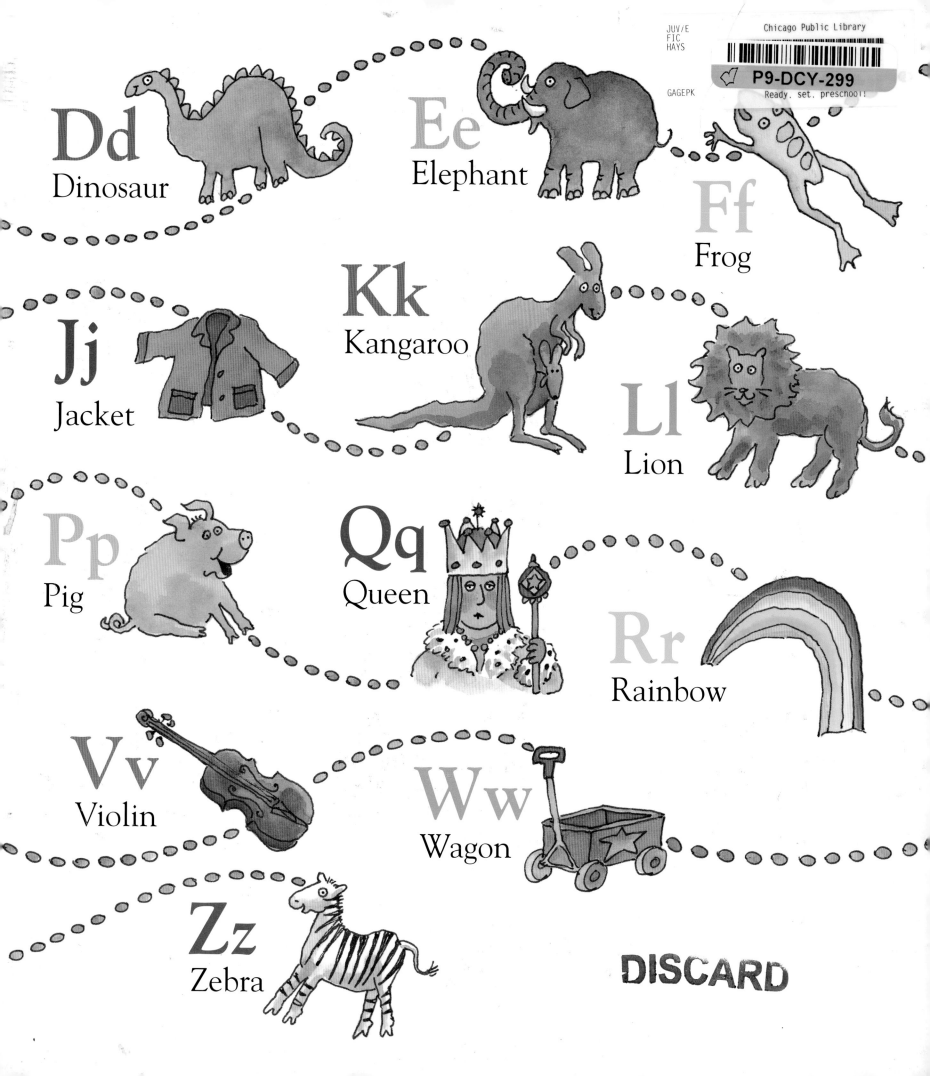

READY, SET, PRESCHOOL!

By **Anna Jane Hays**

Illustrated by **True Kelley**

oops!

AARON

SHELBY

KOKO

JESSICA

ALFRED A. KNOPF 🐎 NEW YORK

This book is for Andrew, Shelby, Anna, and Max, with love.
—A.J.H.

For Jane Broadrick, with thanks.
—T.K.

THIS IS A BORZOI BOOK PUBLISHED BY ALFRED A. KNOPF
Text copyright © 2005 by Anna Jane Hays
Illustrations copyright © 2005 by True Kelley

www.randomhouse.com/kids

Library of Congress Cataloging-in-Publication Data
Hays, Anna Jane.
Ready, set, preschool! : stories, poems, and picture games, with an educational guide for parents /
by Anna Jane Hays ; illustrated by True Kelley. — 1st ed.
p.   cm.
"A Borzoi book."
SUMMARY: A collection of simple stories, poems, and picture games
designed to prepare children for preschool.
ISBN 0-375-82519-3 (trade) — ISBN 0-375-92519-8 (lib. bdg.)
I. Kelley, True, ill. II. Title.
PZ7.H314917Re 2005
[E]—dc21   2004019248

MANUFACTURED IN CHINA
July 2005   First Edition
10 9 8 7 6 5 4 3 2

INTRODUCTION

This collection of read-aloud stories, poems, and picture games is designed for the child headed for the exciting new world of preschool—and for the parent who cares to help.

GET READY: The child who knows *what to expect* is ready for the socialization and learning experiences of preschool. This book explores the typical classroom and what may happen there. The child who knows *what will be expected* can prepare for behaviors such as saying goodbye without tears, sharing and taking turns, and using the toilet. The child who knows some *basic skills* can feel capable entering the classroom.

GET SET: Armed with these tools, your child can begin the preschool adventure with confidence. Engage your child in preparations such as buying school shoes and stuffing a backpack with fresh school supplies. Preparations increase anticipation.

In my years at Sesame Street, where preschool preparation is the priority, I saw it demonstrated that children are able to learn more, and at a younger age, than had been believed possible in the past. You can help your preschoolers make the most of this auspicious time. Awaken their awareness to lessons inherent in the world around them. Make a game of finding geometric shapes in nature and architecture, and children will delight in making these discoveries themselves. My own toddler once came running to me with a slice of pizza and shouted, "Mom, look! A *triangle*!"

Be alert to opportunities for counting: "How many dogs is that boy walking?" Call attention to relational concepts *as* your child experiences them—going in or out, up or down; waiting at the beginning, middle, or end of a line. Point out letters, words, and numbers on signs, buildings, and vehicles.

Step back at times and allow children to do things for themselves: brushing, buttoning, pulling on shirts, socks, and shoes. Mastery of small personal tasks gives children the courage to try bigger ones. Reinforce that confidence by acknowledging accomplishments and minimizing failures. There will always be a chance to try again!

Different abilities evolve at different rates, often causing impatience with "growing up." A four-year-old in my family, comparing himself with his six-year-old brother, wailed to his mother, "I can't whistle, I can't snap my fingers, and I can't *read*!" Within the year he could do all three, but not until he had developed physically and intellectually to the point he had reached emotionally at age four.

The **Notes to Parents** in the back of the book explain the educational value of each entry and its specific contribution to preschool readiness. They are to help you interpret and build on the book's content.

As your child prepares to **GO TO PRESCHOOL**, I hope that you take pleasure in sharing these stories, poems, pictures—and the joy of discovery.

—Anna Jane Hays
July 2005

MY NAME IS ANNA

My name is Anna,
Anna is my name.
Backward or forward,
the letters are the same.
There's an A at the beginning
and an *a* just where it ends,
and squeezed right in the middle
are two little *n*'s.

When I go to sleep at night,
Anna is my name.
When I wake up in the morning,
my name is still the same.
My parents call me Anna,
I'm called Anna by my Granna,
my friends say "Anna Banana!"
That's okay with me.
I'm Anna at the playground,
I'm Anna at the zoo,
and when I'm big enough for school,
then I'll be Anna, too!

My name is Anna.
Anna is the name I write
when I write my name.
I take it with me everywhere,
I wear it in my curly hair,
it's written on my underwear.
Call me Martha? Don't you dare!
Anna is my name.

CASEY COUNTS

Casey wants to take his best things to school. Can you count them?

One blankie for quiet time. 1

Two books with words that rhyme.

2

Three race cars that go *zoom-zoom*. 3

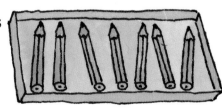

Four grasshoppers to hop in the room. 4

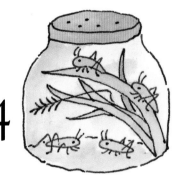

Five notebooks for his writing. 5

Six red apples ripe for biting. 6

Seven pencils in a box. 7

Eight special sparkly rocks. 8

Nine leaves for show-and-tell. 9

Ten crayons that color well. 10

Now Casey is ready to go!

WHAT'S IN THE CLASSROOM?

There are so many exciting new things to see and new friends to make in preschool.
The teacher, Ms. Willson, makes everyone welcome in her classroom.

Aa Bb Cc Dd Ee Ff Gg Hh Ii Jj Kk Ll Mm Nn Oo Pp Qq Rr Ss Tt Uu Vv Ww Xx Yy Zz

plant

alphabet

clock

piano

dinosaur

calendar

bell

chalkboard

desk

1 2 3 4 5 6 7 8 9 10

chair

dog

teacher

boy

girl

easel

turtle

paint

PRETEND

Can you find Casey's things before the school bell rings?

window

door

cubby

book

puzzle

sink

blocks

box

table

7

QUACK LIKE A DUCK! MOO LIKE A COW!

Today Ms. Willson takes the class to visit a farm.
Say the words for the pictures in the poem and do what the animal does.
Say what the animal says!

You lucky
Paddle and splash
forward and back.
QUACK! QUACK! QUACK!

Now be a
and chew, chew, chew.
What does the cow say?
MOO! MOO! MOO!

Be a baby
Hatch and scratch.
Peck and peep.
CHEEP! CHEEP! CHEEP!

8

Be a proud
and trot, trot, trot!
What does the horse say?
NEIGH! NEIGH!

Stretch like a
and lick your paws.
Cry like a cat. How?
MEOW! MEOW!

Be a busy bumble
Fly from flower to flower.
Do what the bee does,
BUZZ! BUZZ! BUZZ!

UNDER THE RAINBOW

After the rain, children come out to play under the rainbow.

Can you find something in the playground that matches every color in the rainbow?

Aaron's favorite color is red.

Can you guess other children's favorite colors?

What is your favorite color?

RED

ORANGE

YELLOW

GREEN

BLUE

PURPLE

KATIE CAN DO IT!

Guess what, Elizabeth. I'm going to go to school.
Because I'm a big girl. You are still a baby.

I can do lots of things you can't do yet.
I go in the potty!
I wear big-girl pants. See?
So when I have to go, I just pull them
down and sit on the potty.
Going in the potty is very important.
You still go in your diapers.

Know what else I can do? I can button my dress.
I buttoned all of these buttons by myself.
You don't even have buttons. You have baby snaps.

And I can put on my shoes and fasten
them up. One strap goes this way and
the other strap goes that way. Then
I stick them down tight like this.
You are too little to wear shoes.

You know what else? I can put on my jacket all by myself. I know a jacket trick. It's a secret, but I'll show you if you promise not to tell. I lay the jacket down flat and stick my arms in the sleeves from the top. Then I just flip it over my head.

Like this!

Putting on a jacket is very important.

I can write my name. See? It says KATIE. You can't read it yet, but that's what it says. In school I will learn to write Katherine.

Now I have to go to the bathroom. I'll go in the potty. When I'm done, I'll wipe, and flush, and wash my hands with soap. Someday you'll be a big girl, too, and know how to go in the potty. You wait here, Elizabeth. When I come out, I'll read you a story.

SHAPES ROUND-UP

The preschool class visits the Triangle-Square Ranch!

Can you help round up shapes?

Look at the shapes at the top of the page and find them hiding in the picture.

TRIANGLE SQUARE CIRCLE RECTANGLE

AARON CAN'T WAIT

Aaron can't wait for the first day of school. Then he'll wear his new school shoes. He'll make new friends and show them his moon rock. Aaron can't wait!

Finally, the big day came. Aaron put on his new school shoes. He put his moon rock in his pocket. And he walked to school with his daddy.

The teacher, Ms. Willson, met Aaron and his daddy at the door of the classroom. She showed Aaron his own cubby for his backpack and jacket.

Then he and Daddy walked around the classroom. They saw big blocks stacked against the wall and shelves of picture books.

A piano was in one corner and a big basket was in another. "This is our Let's Pretend corner," said Ms. Willson.

Outside the window they could see the playground with monkey bars and a seesaw.

"This looks okay, right, Aaron?" his daddy asked. Aaron nodded yes. "So I guess I'll go now," said his daddy.

"Where are you going?" asked Aaron. "We have to go to school."

"*You* are going to school and *I* am going to work," said his daddy. "We talked about this yesterday, Aaron."

Aaron looked around the room at all the children. He didn't know any of them.

"Don't go, Daddy," he whispered.

Just then Ms. Willson came over, bringing another boy. "Aaron," she said, "this is Shelby. He has something to show you."

"I have a conch shell from the bottom of the ocean," said Shelby.

"I have a rock that looks like it came from the moon," said Aaron.

He took his moon rock out of his pocket and held it out. Shelby let Aaron hold his big shell. Then they began building a fort with blocks around the seashell and the moon rock.

17

"Class is about to begin, boys and girls," said Ms. Willson. "Sit down at a table, please."

Aaron and Shelby ran to a table and sat in chairs near each other.

Aaron's daddy came over and gave Aaron a hug. "I have to go now," he said. "But Red Ted can stay. And I'll be back to pick you up at three o'clock."

Aaron made a face.

"Goodbye," said Daddy.

Aaron said nothing.

Shelby's mommy came over and hugged him goodbye.

"Bye, Mommy," said Shelby.

"Bye, Daddy," said Aaron at last. He opened a notebook on the table. "Can you write your name?" he asked Shelby.

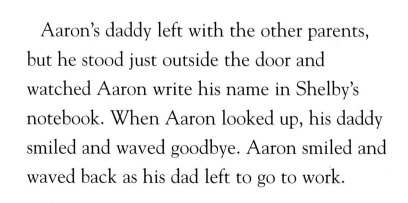

Aaron's daddy left with the other parents, but he stood just outside the door and watched Aaron write his name in Shelby's notebook. When Aaron looked up, his daddy smiled and waved goodbye. Aaron smiled and waved back as his dad left to go to work.

Aaron's daddy came back to the school at three o'clock.

"Time to go home, Aaron!" he said. But Aaron wasn't ready to leave. He and Anna were stacking blocks neatly against the wall. Shelby and Katie were putting picture books back on the bookshelves.

Aaron showed his daddy the painting he had made. Finally, Aaron packed up his backpack and was ready to go. He said goodbye to Ms. Willson. He said goodbye to Shelby.

Walking home from school with his daddy, Aaron said, "I can't wait for school—tomorrow!"

CATCH KOKO!

Koko snatched Shelby's sneaker and dived UNDER his bed.
Shelby crawled after her and—*bonk!*—bumped his head.

Koko ran UP the stairs and scared the napping cat.
Then she tumbled DOWN the stairs and mashed Shelby's hat.

Koko raced across the floor BETWEEN Daddy's feet
and jumped OVER the sofa with Granny in her seat.

She tore AROUND the table, upsetting Mother's plate,
and jumped THROUGH the window
and ran OUT the gate!
Shelby chased her, calling,
"STOP, KOKO! WAIT!"

But Koko just kept going, right IN the muddy pond,
then *splish-splashed* OUT again on the bank beyond.

Koko stopped to shiver and shake—
and that's when Shelby got his break!

"NOW I'VE GOT YOU, KOKO!"
Then what did Shelby do?
He put ON his shoe.

WILL I HAVE A FRIEND?

Today was Jessica's first day at her new preschool.

Her family had just moved to the neighborhood, and school had already started. Jessica thought about her friends at her old school.

"Will I have a friend at my new school?" she asked her mother.

"You'll make new ones!" her mother said.

Jessica wasn't so sure.

In Ms. Willson's class, Jessica stood by her cubby and looked around the room. When Ms. Willson asked the boys and girls to sit down, Jessica didn't know anybody to sit next to. When it was time to go to the playground, she didn't have a partner to walk with.

Ms. Willson took Jessica to the playground and showed her the swings.

"Why don't you push Katie until it's your turn? Then she can push you," said Ms. Willson.

So Jessica pushed Katie. Higher and higher, she pushed her. Then Katie jumped out of the swing and pushed Jessica. Higher and higher. It was fun!

But when Jessica's turn was over, Katie called to her friend Anna and ran over to her.

Jessica sat down on the seesaw and watched. Everybody had a friend—everybody but Jessica.

Suddenly . . . *Whish! Whomp!* She flew up in the air on the seesaw! Then she heard somebody laughing. It was a big kid sitting on the other end of the seesaw.

He was on the ground. Jessica was sitting on the end high up in the air, her legs dangling.

"Hey!" she said. "Let me down!"
"What do you say?" he said.
Jessica thought for a minute.

"Please?" she said.

Whomp! Her end of the seesaw hit the ground and bounced. The big kid had jumped off and was running toward the monkey bars.

"Hey, wait!" called Jessica. "Let's seesaw together."

The boy came back and climbed on the seesaw near the middle. Then he rode up while Jessica rode down. Up and down, up and down they seesawed. It was fun!

"My name is Jessica," she said. "You can call me Jessie."

"Okay," he said. "My name is Casey."

They seesawed until Ms. Willson called the class in for lunch. Now Jessica had a partner—Casey.

When they opened their lunchboxes, Casey saw Jessie's lunch. "Wow!" he said. "I love marshmallow crispy squares. Want to share? I have chocolate-chip cookies and a peanut-butter and banana sandwich."

"I love peanut-butter and banana!" said Jessica.

So Jessica gave Casey half her tuna and carrot sandwich and one marshmallow crispy square, and Casey gave Jessica half his peanut-butter and banana sandwich and a chocolate-chip cookie.

After lunch they built a ranch with blocks.

They shared a paint box and painted two pictures.

They sat together at story time.

When Casey's mother came to the classroom to pick him up, Jessie was surprised that the school day was over so soon.

"What are you bringing for lunch tomorrow?" Casey asked.

"The same," said Jessie. "Want to share?"

"Sure," he said. "Want to have a playdate tomorrow?"

"Sure," she said.

Then Jessica's mother arrived.

Jessica ran over to her. "Guess what," she said. "I have a new friend!"

LET'S PRETEND

What's in the Let's Pretend basket?

Use your imagination and be whatever you want to be!

THE NEW SHOES

Look at the pictures and tell a story.

And then what happened?

THE PARTS OF ME

I like to wash the parts of me
that everybody else can see,
my hands and ears and one skinned knee,
my face and mouth that say I'm me.
I wash the parts nobody knows
'cause they were covered by my clothes,
my belly button, chest and toes,
and back and tummy, all of those.
When I am finally clean, I say,
"Nighty-night!" and right away
dream of messy ways to play.
Tomorrow is another day!

NOTES TO PARENTS

ALPHABET, Front Endpaper
• THE ALPHABET
A to Z, the alphabet is the code to reading.

The first step in mastery of the alphabet is to say it or sing it. It is easier to learn in the rhythm and rhyme of an alphabet song.

The second step is visual recognition of the capital and small letters and naming them. Then it is just a hop to the sound the letter represents and a skip to associating that sound with words. Letters are symbols for sounds, and words are symbols for the things they represent.

Look at the alphabet in the front endpaper of this book and say the names of the letters with your child, first in sequence and eventually at random. Then point out the picture with each letter and demonstrate that the word for it begins with the sound of that letter.

MY NAME IS ANNA, page 4
• IDENTITY, SELF-ESTEEM
A child's first bit of self-knowledge is his or her name. It is often the first word a baby responds to and the first word a child can read and write.

Anna is proud of her name because she knows it stands for herself, wherever she goes. Talk to your child about his or her own name and particular traits.

Self-esteem and a strong sense of self are invaluable assets for the child to take to school. Pride in themselves gives children the confidence to tackle new challenges and be receptive to learning.

CASEY COUNTS, page 5
NUMBERS, Back Endpaper
• NUMBERS AND COUNTING
First your child learns to recite the numbers 1 to 10 and recognize them visually. Then the child can call the numbers by name, and is ready to count. Counting is relating the concept of "how many" to a number.

With your child, look at Casey's things and point out the numbers. Then ask your child to point to one thing after another within each group while saying the numbers in sequence. Explain that the last number tells "how many"— and that is counting.

Your child can practice with the numbers on the endpaper in the back of this book.

WHAT'S IN THE CLASSROOM?, pages 6-7
• COUNTING, VOCABULARY
Counting Casey's things in the classroom is a more sophisticated task because the child must find them first in the busy scene. The icons at the top of the page are a guide for matching and counting these objects. Make a game of it and encourage the searching and counting only as long as your child is interested.

Familiarity with a typical preschool classroom like Ms. Willson's helps the child feel more prepared to enter this world. Knowing what to expect—and the vocabulary for it— helps the child feel ready and able.

You can help your child learn classroom words. Read the labels out loud, and then have your child point in the picture to answer your questions: Where is the teacher? Is there a piano in the classroom? Do any animals go to school?

Enrich vocabulary further by making a practice of calling attention to things by name. And when your child gestures instead of speaking, suggest, "Use your words!"

QUACK LIKE A DUCK! MOO LIKE A COW!, pages 8-9
• SOUNDS, WORDS, AND RHYME
Words that imitate noises are fun for children to say and demonstrate sounds becoming words. It is a short step from sounds *as* words to sounds *in* words. Phonics is the sound/word relationship of reading.

Rhyming stories and poems reinforce this awareness. As you read these verses, have your child say the animal's name for each rebus picture. When you get to the animal's sound, point out the word and ask your child to "read" it out loud. The animal sounds rhyme in the verses.

UNDER THE RAINBOW, pages 10-11
COLORS, Back Endpaper

• **COLORS** Recognizing colors by sight and by name can be learned very young. You can build on that knowledge by helping your child become aware of the colors that paint our world: in nature, in our surroundings, in art.

Talk about the colors in the game "Under the Rainbow" and on the endpaper in the back of the book.

Call colors by name wherever you see them. And when you happen to see a rainbow arcing joyfully over the horizon, point out how the colors always appear magically in order: red, orange, yellow, green, blue, and purple.

KATIE CAN DO IT!, pages 12-13

• **THE POTTY AND SELF-HELP**

The child who can use the potty or toilet starts school with a big advantage. Many preschools do not admit children wearing diapers. Children are asked to wear pull-ups or training pants and bring an extra pair in their backpacks.

Sooner or later, children understand that everybody goes to the bathroom and that the bathroom is the place to go. The habit will be reinforced in school with peers who use the toilet.

Children adapt to the toilet when they are ready, but you can foster this readiness by encouraging self-sufficiency. Let your child perform self-help tasks such as putting on jackets and pants, buttoning and zipping clothes. These accomplishments can translate into capability in other areas of the child's daily life, such as going to the bathroom.

Katie's ability to do many things for herself makes her more confident and ready for school.

SHAPES ROUND-UP, pages 14-15

• **SHAPES**

At this preschool point in your child's career, recognition of shapes is a plus. It employs the same visual discrimination skill used to identify letters and numbers.

The small shapes above the Triangle-Square Ranch scene are models for the child to use in playing the game of matching the shapes embedded in the picture.

You can help your child find shapes in the real world: rec-tangle doors, square windows, circle manhole covers, triangle traffic signs, etc. Children delight in these discoveries when they become alert to seeing shapes. It's satisfying also for children to find shapes in paintings and sculptures, and to use shapes in making their own art.

AARON CAN'T WAIT, pages 16-19

• **SEPARATION**

Saying goodbye is more difficult when children don't understand that there will be an end of the separation and a hello. Children need reassurance that the parent will return. Talk about where you are going and when you will be back. Talk about the things your child can enjoy in your absence. Explain in advance, and discuss it again just before the event.

As your child braves the new world of school, send along something familiar and comforting, such as a doll or teddy bear or blanket.

Aaron couldn't wait for the first day of school, but when it arrived he didn't want his dad to leave. See that your child is engaged in an activity before you go. Once you've said goodbye, don't linger long. Finally, don't be surprised at ambivalent feelings of your own, and try not to let them show as you make a cheery departure.

CATCH KOKO!, pages 20-21

• **OPPOSITES, RELATIONAL CONCEPTS**

Koko the puppy races through situations that demonstrate relational concepts. To be understood by young children, opposites and physical relationship to place must be seen in concrete examples.

Read the story poem to your child and look at the overview of Koko's path together. The child can use a finger to trace the puppy's escape route from beginning to end. Make a game out of finding the places where relational concepts occur. Ask questions: "Where does Koko go UP the stairs?" "Does Koko run AROUND anyone?" "Where does Koko get OUT?"

Understanding opposites and relational concepts develops children's perspective of the world and their place in it.

WILL I HAVE A FRIEND?, pages 22-25
• MAKING FRIENDS, SOCIALIZATION

For the child just starting school or moving to a new school, a classroom of so many children can be overwhelming. No matter how positive your approach, preschool presents new challenges. Before school starts, introduce strategies for getting along, such as sharing, taking turns, and cooperating. At first, such democratic concepts may be difficult to embrace because toddlers are the center of their worlds.

Making friends in school is necessary for adapting to this new, wider world. It's easier through a common interest, trading lunch treats, or cooperative play.

In the months leading up to school, nurture positive anticipation. Talk about the adventures in store with new playmates, playthings, and powers such as reading and writing!

LET'S PRETEND, pages 26-27
• CREATIVITY AND IMAGINATION

Perhaps creativity can't be taught, but it can be stimulated and nurtured. Encourage the creative inclination with paint and craft materials. Provide opportunities for children to make their own play and playthings. A Let's Pretend basket is a rich resource for fantasy and improvisation. Make everyday stuff available for children to transform into props and costumes for imaginative play. Discovering the many possibilities of things opens the mind to fresh ways of thinking and problem solving.

Making up new roles is constructive, creative work for kids. When they pretend—through personification, dolls, or puppets—children are interpreting their world and working out problems. Imaginative play can be a vehicle for expressing emotions that might be difficult to articulate. And expanding the imagination widens the world of options.

THE NEW SHOES, pages 28-29
• STORYTELLING

"And then what happened?" Ask this as your child follows the pictures and makes up the story. If necessary, ask leading questions: "What does she want in the store?" "Why is she crying?" Then let your child's imagination fly. Storytelling is self-expression to be respected. Listen to the narrative, and listen between the lines. You may learn something about your child's feelings and perceptions.

Making up stories is a giant step toward reading and writing. It is valuable experience for a pre-reader to organize events into a narrative with a beginning, a middle, and (perhaps) an end.

Encourage your child to tell stories. Call attention to people or events and ask what is happening, or what could happen. Then your child might like to "write" that story with crayon pictures and scribble.

Storytelling paves the way to reading and writing while suggesting sequence and increasing vocabulary.

THE PARTS OF ME, page 30
• PARTS OF THE BODY

Self-knowledge begins with the body. Young children need to learn the names of the parts of their bodies, and how to use them and clothe them.

You can reinforce these facts when a child is dressing or bathing.

It is for you to decide when to introduce genital vocabulary and what words to use. You will establish how body parts and functions are defined in your family, whether in diminutives, euphemisms, or anatomical terms. It's important for children to know about their bodies and to understand that their bodies are private and belong to themselves.

Red

Purple

Yellow

Black

Orange

White

Blue

Brown

Green

Pink